Usborne First Experiences

Going to School Sticker Book

Anna Civardi

Illustrated by Stephen Cartwright

Edited by Kirsteen Rogers

How to use this book

Some words in this story have been replaced by pictures.
Find the stickers that match these pictures and stick them over the top.
Each sticker has the word with it to help you read the story.

Some of the big pictures have pieces missing.
Find the stickers with the missing pieces to finish the pictures.

A yellow duck is hidden in every picture. When you have found
the duck you can put a ![I found the duck!] sticker on the page.

This is the Peach family.

Mrs. Peach

Mr. Peach

Polly
Peach

Sidney
the gerbil

Percy
Peach

Pong
the
kitten

Ping
the other kitten

Dusty the cat

Percy and Polly are twins. Tomorrow is their first

day at school. Polly has a brand new  bag

and Percy has a yellow spotted .

The Peaches live above the Marsh family.

"Hello, Millie," calls Percy from the  .

"Hello. I'm so excited about school. Are you?" asks

Millie. "Yes. And I've got a !" he says.

3

Mr. and Mrs. Peach wake Percy and Polly.

"Wake up, Sleepyhead!" says Mrs. Peach. "It's

time for school. I've got your  here. Red

 or blue? Look, Polly is almost dressed!"

After breakfast they brush their teeth.

Then the twins put on their  and

. Millie and her Dad pop their

head around the door. "Are you ready?" they say.

5

They all walk to school together.

There are  everywhere. Polly feels

shy and keeps her  on. "You can stay for

a while, Mrs. Peach," says Mrs. Todd, the teacher.

6

They hang up their coats.

Mr. Peach hangs Percy's  on his own

special peg. "No, Percy, I'm afraid Sidney the

 must come home with me," he says.

Percy and Polly join their class.

There are lots of things to do. Some children are

painting  , some are dressing up,

and there are plenty of  to look at.

8

I found the duck!

fruit

I found the duck!

piano

scissors

shoes

hoops

I found the duck!

triangle

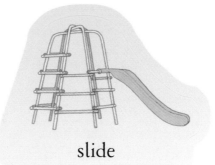
slide

t-shirt

bananas

gerbil

coat

I found the duck!

children

I found the duck!

glue

book

I found the duck!

tiger

I found the duck!

window

socks

I found the duck!

I found the duck!

lunchbox

children

clothes

pictures

cups

coat

I found the duck!

bucket

lunchbox

I found the duck!

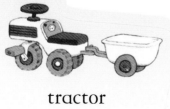
tractor

clothes

I found the duck!

coats

books

I found the duck!

A group of children are making masks, with paper,

 and . Two girls are playing

with clay. What are Percy and Polly doing?

9

They have fun making things.

Two teachers help the  to make

tiny washing lines full of paper  .

"Glue on the paper, please, Percy!" says Miss Joss.

10

Next, it's music time.

Miss Dot, the music teacher, plays the

and teaches them lots of songs. Millie tinkles

a and Polly jingles a tambourine.

At 11 o'clock, it's time for a snack.

There are of juice for everyone as

well as a big bowl of and a plate of

cookies. Percy and Polly are hungry and thirsty.

Now it's story time.

"Sit down, please, everyone," says Mrs. Judd,

opening a big  . "Today's story is about

a  . Look this way, please, Percy."

The children go out into the playground.

They find lots of things to play with. There's

a big climbing frame, as well as balls,

bicycles and even a toy  .

Polly loves going down the . Percy

is playing with a  of sand. Can

you see what Milly has found to play with?

Soon it's time to go home.

"Look at the paper  I made!" says Polly.

"I ate two and I've made lots of friends."